HERGÉ

THE ADVENTURES OF TINTIN

RED RACKHAM'S
TREASURE

Translated by Leslie Lonsdale-Cooper
and Michael Turner

Artwork copyright © 1945 by Éditions Casterman, Tournai.
Copyright © renewed 1973 by Casterman.
Library of Congress Catalogue Card Numbers Afor 813 and R 558597
Text © 1959 by Egmont Children's Books Ltd.
First published in Great Britain in 1959.
Reprinted 1965 and 1968
Reprinted six times by Methuen Children's Books Ltd.
Published as a paperback in 1974
Reprinted as a Magnet paperback 1978
Reprinted nine times
Reissued 1990 by Mammoth,
an imprint of Egmont Children's Books Limited
239 Kensington High Street, London W8 6SL

Reprinted 1992, 1993 (twice), 1994, 1995 (twice), 1996, 1997, 1998, 2001 (twice), 2002.

Printed in Spain by Edelvives
ISBN 0-7497-0463-2

RED RACKHAM'S
TREASURE

'Morning.

Ahoy there!.. Bill!...

Hello, George! How's yourself?...

Not so bad. And you?... Still a ship's cook?

Still the same. I'm sailing aboard the SIRIUS in a few days, with Captain Haddock and Tintin. Know them?

Tintin?... Captain Haddock?... I certainly do. There's been plenty of talk about them- over that business of the Bird brothers.[1] But the SIRIUS — she's a trawler, isn't she? Are you going fishing?...

Yes, but it's not ordinary fish we're after, it's treasure!

What's that you say?

Well, it's like this... There's a treasure that belonged to a pirate, Red Rackham, who was killed long ago by Sir Francis Haddock aboard a ship called the UNICORN. Tintin and Captain Haddock found some old parchments...

...written by Sir Francis... who escaped from the ship...They know just where the UNICORN sank and.... I'll tell you the rest later. These walls have ears.

[1] See The Secret of the Unicorn

Red Rackham's Treasure

THE forthcoming departure of the trawler *Sirius* is arousing speculation in sea-faring circles. Despite the close secrecy which is being maintained, our correspondent understands that the object of the voyage is nothing less than a search for treasure.

This treasure, once the hoard of the pirate Red Rackham, lies in the ship *Unicorn*, sunk at the end of the seventeenth century. Tintin, the famous reporter—whose sensational intervention in the Bird case made headline news—and his friend Captain Haddock, have discovered the exact resting-place of the *Unicorn*,

Mr. Tintin ?...

Yes.

Mr. Tintin, I see from this morning's paper that you are going to try and find Red Rackham's treasure. Is that so?

Yes, it is. But...

Good. In that case, I shall accompany you!... As for the treasure, I shall be satisfied with a half share... Here is my card...

!

Is... is that really your name?...

So it seems, young man.

Look, Captain...

Blistering barnacles!

RED RACKHAM

But, if I'm not mistaken, sir, your name is simply Rackham. 'Red' is just a nickname. In which case I see no connection between you and Red Rackham the pirate...

RRRING

Mr. Tintin?... I demand my share of the treasure!... I am Red Rackham's sole descendant!...

Excuse me! I am!

He's not. I am!

It's me!

Don't listen! I'm the one!

I am! And here's my family tree!

Leave this to me! We'll soon see if there's a real Rackham among that crew!

You're all descendants of Red Rackham are you?

Good! Well, I'm descended from Sir Francis Haddock, who killed Red Rackham in single combat... and blew up his ship... And there are times...

...when my ancestor's fighting blood begins to boil!

Avast, freshwater pirates!

What's going on up there?

What a stampede!

Like a lot of wild elephants!

A real herd of elephants!

To be precise: a real herd of elephants!

And there are your records, fancy-dress freebooters!

There you are. That's got rid of that gang of thieves!

RRRRING

Another?

Wait, I'll go ...

Is that you Tintin?... It's us, Thomson and Thompson. Could you give us a hand?... A wild elephant dropped something on our heads.

!

Come in; we'll see to that...

RRRING

?

I'd like to speak to Mr. Tintin.

Why?... No doubt your name happens to be Red Rackham?

Yes?

No, I'm asking you if you're called Red Rackham...

Oh?

WHAT'S YOUR NAME?

Please speak a bit louder. I'm a little hard of hearing.

YOUR NAME!

Gone away?... What a pity! Never mind, I'll come again. I particularly wanted to speak to Mr. Tintin himself. ...

I'm Tintin. What do you want?

Ah, Mr. Tintin!... They told me that you were away.

I'm delighted to meet you. My name is Calculus; Cuthbert Calculus.

Oh?

No, Calculus, Cuthbert Calculus. Mr. Tintin, I understand you are setting off on a search for treasure. That's nice. But have you considered the sharks?

The sharks?

No, young man, I'm talking about the sharks. I expect you intend to do some diving. In which case, beware of sharks!

But...

Don't you agree?... But I've invented a machine for underwater exploration, and it's shark-proof. If you'll come to my house with me, I'll show it to you.

I'm very sorry but...

No, it's not far. Less than ten minutes...

I'm afraid I'm very busy and I...

Why of course. Certainly these gentlemen may come too.

It's no good. There's no time! NO TIME!

Good, that's settled. We'll go at once.

I'm so glad you agreed to come!

Please don't mention it.

No, Calculus, Cuthbert Calculus.

You see, here we are. One more floor...

It's in here...

Yes, that's a new device for putting bubbles in soda-water...

And that's a clothes brushing machine.

Not a bad gadget, eh?

No, a clothes-brushing machine. It's one of my latest inventions.

RRRR ✶ OUCH ✶

OW ✶

OOH ✶

The clothes are sucked into the middle of the machine, where they have a stiff brushing for half a minute. Then they come out, as good as new...

Billions of bilious blistering barnacles!!

Let me go! I'll tell him what I think of his practical joke!

You're going to buy me a new outfit, do you hear?

That?... Yes, it's for brushing clothes.

But this is even more ingenious. Because I have so little room and my bed gets in the way...

...I designed the wall-bed.

You Bashi-bazouk! Look what you've done now!

You bragging nitwit, you! Look!

How do I close it up again? There...

Between ourselves, I wouldn't have expected such childish pranks from them. They looked quite sensible...

And here's my apparatus for exploring the sea-bed.

As you can see for yourselves, it's a kind of small submarine. It is powered by an electric motor, and has oxygen supplies for two hours' diving...

Now I'll show you how the apparatus works...

? CRACK

I can't understand it!...It's sabotage! No sir, I said it's sabotage!... Someone has sabotaged my machine!

We are extremely sorry, Professor Calculus, extremely sorry, but your machine will not do.

For two? You'd like a two-seater?

8

No, Professor Calculus, I said your machine won't do for us!

Oh, good!

Well, gentlemen, that's agreed. I'll make another smaller one. It will be ready in eight days' time...

Some days later...

Well, we're all ready to start – at least, if we can find a diving-suit. I've spent three days hunting through marine stores, and I still haven't unearthed one.

I say, look there!

Great snakes! Let's go and see...

FOR SALE
Complete Diving Equipment, as new

We'd like to see the diving equipment, please.

The diving-suit? Please follow me.

There...

Beware, young fellow, beware! Money is the root of all evil!

?

Why... why do you say that?

Why?... Because I see that you intend to go treasure-hunting...

You see that? Where can you see it?

I read it in your face.

In my face?... But...but ...what's unusual about my face? Tintin, can you see anything?

Well, I...

Blistering barnacles!

It's horrible!... What's happened to me?...

Nothing, Captain! It's just that you were looking in a concave mirror! And here's a convex one!

Thank goodness!

But here's another mirror... I'll just reassure myself!

Oh!

Seven years of bad luck!

And two pounds for the mirror!

You can take it from me: I'm telling you the truth: there's no such thing as buried treasure nowadays...

Never mind that. How much is the diving-suit?

Ten pounds.

All right. We'll have it collected this afternoon. Shall we go, Captain?

Remember what I said, my lad. You won't find any treasure!

Next day...

SIRIUS

Good morning, Captain. All well?

No, bad!

Yes, bad. Very bad... I'm ill... 'Flu, I expect... And I've been thinking... I... well... briefly, to put it in a nutshell, I'm not going!

!

You can't be serious!

Perfectly serious. I'm not superstitious, but to break a mirror on the eve of a voyage... No, definitely, I'm not going!

Hello!

Bad news, my friends. We've just heard that Max Bird has escaped!

What did I tell you?... A good start, isn't it? ...

Yes, that troublesome antique dealer—he managed to give two policemen the slip when he was being taken for questioning.

That's bad...

There's a letter for you, Captain.

For me?...What's this about?

Billions of bilious blue blistering barnacles!

Is it bad news, Captain?

Read for yourself! It's ghastly!

DOCTOR A. LEECH

Dear Captain,
I have considered your case, and conclude that your illness is due to poor liver condition.
You must therefore undergo the following treatment:
DIET - STRICTLY FORBIDDEN:
All acoholic beverages (wine, beer, cider, spirits, cocktails,

Good-day, gentlemen! I hope I'm not intruding?

No? Well, I'm happy to tell you my machine is ready now. When may I come aboard?

You can't come aboard! We aren't interested in your machine!

Tomorrow?

No not tomorrow! Never!

Today?... Good. I'll go and fetch it at once.

At last we are on our way, Snowy.

Tintin!

A radio message...

"Port Commander to Captain SIRIUS. Reduce speed. Motor boat coming out to you."

What can this mean?

Look!... There's a motor-boat coming now.

I can't quite see the passenger; but it'd better not be Professor Calculus!

Thomson and Thompson! What are they coming aboard for?

Hello! We're coming with you!

Coming with us?...

Yes, we've had orders to protect you.

Protect us? Is someone threatening us?...

Yes, you are in danger. Max Bird, the antique dealer, was seen last night skulking near the SIRIUS. He may try to take his revenge.

Just let him try! He'll find out...

Maybe, maybe. But anyway, now we are aboard you will be able to feel that you are perfectly safe.

To be precise: perfectly safe.

We shall see... Meanwhile we must find you a berth. Let's see... We've a couple of spare bunks for'ard. Will that do?

Yes, thanks!

Captain!... Captain!

Captain, I can't stand it!

What?

This thieving Snowy- he's stolen a whole box of biscuits!

No?...

Snowy?...

Yes, Snowy! I saw him just now near the galley!

Snowy!...Where is the wretched animal?

Snowy?... SNOWY?...

I can't see him, the scoundrel! But don't worry, I'll see that it doesn't happen again...

Good.

Er...our cabin is for'ard, isn't it?

Yes   for'ard.

We'll change at once, and mix discreetly with the ship's company...

Good   idea!

We must behave like old sea-dogs ...

For a start, we'd better learn to chew tobacco. All old sea-dogs chew a quid. Here, have one of these...

What do we do, Captain? We're bearing down on that fishing fleet...

Give a blast on the siren; that'll warn them.

TOOOOOT

Goodness!... My tobacco!..

Mine... mine too ... I swallowed it!...

Next day ...

This has got to stop!... Yes, it's got to stop!

Yes, Captain. Yesterday it was a box of biscuits! This morning a whole chicken has disappeared!

The wretched dog!

Snowy ! ... Snowy ! ... Where's he hiding? ... Snowy !

Snowy!... Snowy!...

Snowy!... Snowy!... Where on earth can he be hid------ing?...

You really saw him make off with the chicken?

Well, I didn't exactly see him, but I supposed...

You supposed!... You supposed!... Don't you accuse anyone of anything unless you have proof!... Besides, how do we know you didn't eat the chicken yourself?...

That evening...

Good night. You might just keep an eye on Snowy.

Don't worry, I'll watch him! Good night, Captain...

THIEF!

SAME TO YOU

Crumbs! That's the two detectives...

What's going on here?...

! !

It's him, Tintin!... He's stolen my pillow!

That's not true! It's him—he's taken one of my blankets!

Aren't you ashamed, at your age? Quarrelling over such trifles! Now, that's all over, isn't it?

Now let's go to bed!

Billions of blistering barnacles!

?

What's the matter, Captain?

The matter?. Blistering barnacles, my bottle of whisky has vanished!

Vanished? Someone must be worried about your health and is keeping you to your diet...

You can laugh! ...But if I catch the crook, he's in for a rough time!

We'll investigate it in the morning. Now let's go to bed. I'm dead tired. Good night!

You go to sleep if you like. I know what I'm going to do.

Thundering typhoons!

THUMP THUMP THUMP

Tintin, Tintin, come quickly!... There's not a moment to lose!...

We're going to blow up!... There's a bomb in the hold!...

I went down to the hold to open a case of whisky. And instead of whisky I found a bomb there! ...

Here we are... Careful!

In here... Look...

Careful!...Don't go near it!

I must. We've got to get to the bottom of this ...

Well?...

Steel plates!

Steel plates?...

You're right, by thunder! ... Then it's not a bomb after all?...

Definitely not. Look, we'll open another case...

Blistering barnacles! More steel plates!

And in this one...

More steel plates!

Steaming blood! There's not a drop of whisky aboard! If I catch the monster who played this trick on us, he'll be in for a rough time!...

Come on, Captain. We'll try and solve this mystery in the morning...

Next day...

Anyway, we can't accuse Snowy any more. Some biscuits, even a chicken perhaps. But not a bottle of whisky!

18

OH!

Great snakes!... He... he... why, he's drunk!

Snowy, what have you done? Pooh! Your breath smells of whisky!

Now come on!... Show us where you found the whisky...

All right... You... you want a d-d-d-drink too?

? ?

Look!

See, the bottle must have smashed up there. Let's investigate.

There!

Blistering barnacles! If I ever catch him!

Sh!... Listen...

ZZZ ...ZZZ... ZZZ ...

Someone is asleep in this life-boat!

Impossible: the lashings are secure ...At least...

Blistering barnacles! The lashings are free this side! There's someone in this life-boat!

! | Thundering typhoons!

ZZZ... ZZZ ...ZZZ...

BISCUITS

Billions of bilious blue blistering barnacles! Get up, you!...

My whisky, you wretch!... What have you done with my whisky? Thundering typhoons, answer me!... Where's my whisky?

I must confess, I did sleep rather badly. But I hope you will give me a cabin...

A cabin!... I'll give you a cabin!...I'm going to stow you in the bottom of the hold for the rest of the voyage, on dry bread and water!... And my whisky?... Where's my whisky?

It's on board, of course!

It's on board!... Heaven be praised!

Naturally it is in separate pieces...

In separate pieces... My whisky is in separate pieces?

Of course, it is a little smaller than the first one, but nevertheless it was too big to pass unnoticed. So I had to dismantle it and pack all the parts in the cases...

But what about the whisky out of those cases! Tell me! Is it still ashore?...

Oh no!

No, no. It was the night before you sailed. The cases were still on the quay, ready to be embarked. I took out all the bottles they contained, and put the pieces of my machine in their place...

Wretch!...Ignoramus! ... Abominable Snowman! ... I'll throw you overboard! Overboard, d'you hear?...

Thank you, Captain, thank you very much! It's just what I expected from you... Such a kind welcome! You'll see – you won't regret it.

Some days later...

Look. We have reached the position indicated by the parchments. We should soon see the island off which the UNICORN sank...

Isn't the island marked on any charts?

No, but that sometimes happens with small, unimportant islands. Come on, we'll try to spot it...

I can't see anything yet... Can you?...

Nothing.

Can you see anything?...

Not yet. But there's a bottle of champagne for the first one to sight land!

Over there!

Where's the island?... I can't see anything...

It was, Captain A shark, I know it was! I saw one, I really did!

21

Still no sign... It's very strange...

What's the name of the island?

How should I know?... It's not marked on any of the charts.

Oh?... But you are sure we're near it?

Positive! I plotted the position yesterday at noon.

Yes, I see. But... er... supposing you made a mistake in your calculations...

❗

Oh, so I made a mistake in my calculations, did I?... All right: they're on my table. Go and check them!... Yes, you! Now! Go on! Check them!

Tell me, Captain, was that a fish jumping out of the water just now?

No, it was a grand piano!

Ah, I didn't think it could have been a fish...

A few minutes later...

You must forgive me, Captain, but there really is a little mistake in your calculations. Look, this is where we are, exactly...

You are right... I have made a mistake. Gentlemen, please take off your hats...

Why must we take off our hats, Captain?...

Sh!...

? ?

Now...

But Captain, tell us what you mean...

I mean, gentlemen, that according to your calculations we are now standing inside Westminster Abbey!

Thousands of thundering typhoons! Where's that miserable island got to?

I'm beginning to think Sir Francis Haddock was pulling our legs.

I'm beginning to think so too!

We'll soon see! It's almost noon. We'll take a sight. I'll go and fetch my sextant.

That's it... Let's go in, and I'll work it out...

The figures given in the parchments were latitude 20°37'42" North, longitude 70°52'15" West. Here's our position now; the same latitude, longitude 71° 2' 29" West.

So we've already passed the right point, and yet we saw nothing... I simply can't understand it!

Captain, I think I've got it!

!

What do you mean?

Well, the meridian from which you calculated the degrees of longitude was of course the Greenwich meridian...

You don't suppose I used one in Timbuctoo!

No, wait. Supposing Sir Francis Haddock used a French chart—he easily could have done. Then zero would be on the Paris meridian—and that lies more than two degrees east of Greenwich!

Blistering barnacles, that's an idea! You may be right! Perhaps we are too far to the west. We'll go back on our tracks...

Coxswain at the wheel! ... Helm hard a-port! ... Midships! ... Steer due east.

?

Captain, what is happening? ... We seem to be turning back.

Yes, Professor Calculus, we're turning back.

Oh, that's all right then ... I was afraid we were turning back.

How easy it is to be mistaken. I'd have sworn we'd turned back.

That evening...

There it is at last! Our treasure island!

It's too late to go ashore tonight. We'll drop anchor, and tomorrow we'll explore the island ...

Right! ...

Next morning ...

Haul the boat up the beach. I'm going to reconnoitre.

24

BANG

Crumbs! What's happened to him?

Captain, what was it? Are you hurt?

No. I stubbed my toe against that thing and fell over. That's how the gun went off...

OW! OW!

Keep calm! Keep calm!

YOW!

Here...

YEOW!

YOW! YEOW!

Oh, leave them... Come and help me dig up this piece of wood. It intrigues me.

Hello, what have they found?

These are the remains of the jolly-boat in which Sir Francis Haddock once came ashore on this island...

This certainly proves that we're nearing our goal. Red Rackham's treasure is out there at the bottom of the sea!... But now, shoes on, everyone, and let's carry on!

WOOAH!

That's Snowy!... He ran on ahead!...

? !

Where did you get that bone from Snowy?... Here, show us where you found it.

Blistering barnacles! I bet these are the remains of the pirates killed when the UNICORN blew up!

They can't be, Captain.

If they were, we'd have found them down by the shore. No, look at this spear. It's more likely that they were natives, killed in a fight, and probably eaten on the spot by their enemies.

Eaten?... Do you mean cannibals lived on this island?... Man-eaters?

That's what we're going to find out. Come on.

Ouch! I've got a pebble in my shoe!

You go on. I'll catch you up...

Look!... There!...

An idol!...

Yes, an idol... But... It's incredible

My word! It's meant to be Sir Francis Haddock!

Look at that mouth! His voice must have made an enormous impression on the natives. I can just imagine their faces the first time they heard him shout: "Ration my rum!"

RRRATION MY RRRUM!

What's the matter, Captain?

Who shouted like that?

What?... Wasn't it you?

No, it wasn't me! Thundering typhoons!

Yes, it's Sir Francis Haddock.

RRRATION MY RRRUM!

It came from over there.

Not a soul!

This island is h-h-haunted, Captain. Let's hurry back t-t-to the sh-sh-ship.

To b-b-be precise: I-let's hurry back t-t-to the sh-sh-ship.

Pithecanthropus!... Pockmark!...

Pockmark yourself, you gibbering ghost!

Come out if you dare, Polynesian! ... Cannibal! ... Iconoclast! ...

Nincompoop! ... Ruffian! ... Baboon!

Up there! ...

Baboon!

Squawking popinjay!

Sea-gherkin!

Pickled Herring!

Blistering barnacles! Parrots!!

Yes, parrots! From generation to generation your ancestor's vocabulary has been handed down!

Pockmark! ... Freshwater swabs! ... Bully! ...

Me, a bully? You called me a bully did you? ...

I'll show you what I'm made of!

Here's a coconut to cut your cackle, iconoclasts!

Ooh, my back!

Wait, I'll rub it for you.

Your gun! ... Give me your gun! ... I'm going to turn them into parrot-soup.

That's done it!... They've dropped the gun!... Look, here it comes...

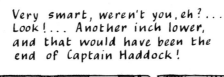

Very smart, weren't you, eh?... Look!... Another inch lower, and that would have been the end of Captain Haddock!

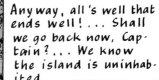

Anyway, all's well that ends well!... Shall we go back now, Captain?... We know the island is uninhabited.

Good idea. Let's go.

Thundering typhoons! I just remembered!

The idol!... Are we going to leave it here?

Ah! what pleasant visions haunt me
As I gaze upon the sea!
All the old romantic legends,
All my dreams, come back
to me . . .

Look out!... A shark!...

Thundering typhoons!... It almost had my hand off!

Look, there's another!... And there... and there ...

Quick, the gun! I'll tell them a thing or two, the brutes!

BING

SIRIUS

You know, Captain, I'm beginning to think Professor Calculus's machine may come in very handy for us...

Next day...

You've made up your mind?

Yes... Professor Calculus has explained exactly how his machine works. It'll be all right...

Stop!... Just a min-ute!...

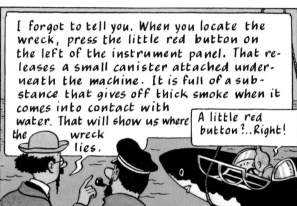
I forgot to tell you. When you locate the wreck, press the little red button on the left of the instrument panel. That releases a small canister attached underneath the machine. It is full of a substance that gives off thick smoke when it comes into contact with water. That will show us where the wreck lies.

A little red button?..Right!

No, red! A little red button ...You've got it? Good... Well, goodbye, and good luck!

There he goes: he's dived.

This is fun, eh Snowy?

Golly, what a lot of water!

Let's hope nothing goes wrong...

Gone long? Why, it's only ten minutes since he dived...

Hello, what's the matter? ... The engine's stopped ... We aren't moving any more!

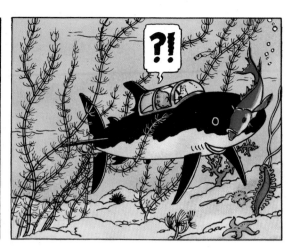
?!

Thing's look bad, Snowy! Our propeller is entangled in the weeds!

We'll try and free ourselves by going into reverse...

It's no good! The propeller is completely jammed... and the engine has stalled!

Well, Snowy my boy, how do we get out of this?

There's only one thing to do: we'll release the smoke-canister. Then at least they'll know where we are... There, we press the little red button here...

That's it...

Look!... Look!... Smoke!... He's found the wreck of the UNICORN!

There, Professor Calculus!... Look!... Smoke!... He's found the wreck!

OH!

Captain, look there!... Look!... No, over there! Smoke!...He's found the wreck!

Patience, Snowy!...It won't be long before someone comes to rescue us.

Ahoy there!...Lower the dinghy!...We'll drop a buoy over the spot Tintin has marked.

There's the buoy...

..And there's the underwater viewing instrument.

It worries me a bit that Tintin hasn't come up again...

No, but I was a great sportsman in my youth...

..And that accounts for the athletic figure I still have..

Hm?...

To be quite honest, no... It was mostly walking...

Let's see...

Thundering typhoons!.. It's not the wreck!... It's Tintin!

Wonderful! Quick, let me look...

Oh, Columbus!...The propeller has been fouled by weeds!... How can we save him?

Really, Captain! Your eyes have deceived you! It's not the wreck, it is Tintin. He can't resurface . . .

Your confounded contraption! I should never have let him go down!

May drown? Well, he had enough oxygen for two hours. He's got... Let's see ... yes, he has just enough for another ten minutes!

I hope they hurry! It's getting more and more difficult to breathe...

What can we do? How can we save him?

Lower a diver?... No, by the time we'd got one equipped and ready, Tintin would be dead...

No, I've got an idea. Take the anchor!... The anchor used for mooring the buoy!

The anchor? What for?...

Of course!... We'll try and hook it on to the submarine. Then we'll pull on the rope until the weeds break...

That's it! Let it down... Lower... lower... lower... gently...

An anchor!... They're going to try to hook me. Quick, empty the ballast tanks, that'll help them...

He's understood. He's emptied the ballast tanks to lighten the submarine... A bit to the left, Captain...Good ... Now, pull!

Ah, they've got it!... I'm saved!... Just in time! I'm suffocating.

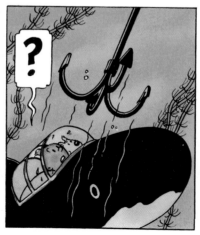

?

Missed!... The anchor hadn't caught properly. Lower it again ... down... stop! A bit to the right... now to the left... Pull it up gently...

Pull!... Pull!... For goodness' sake pull!

Pull!... Go on, pull!

Thundering typhoons, I'm trying to! What do you think I'm doing? Playing the cornet?

Billions of blue blistering barnacles! I hope there aren't any sharks about.

Fresh air!... Fresh air at last!...

Hooray!... He's safe!... Hip-hip-hooray!

All's well!... The Captain has climbed back into the boat... He's salvaged the buoy... hauled the anchor inboard... thrown a lifeline to Tintin... Ah, here they come...

Well, our friend Tintin had a narrow escape!

You are wrong, I assure you. Weeds jammed the propeller. You'll see when we're back on board.

You see?... It's just as I said. Weeds...

Really? I thought they were weeds...

Weeds or no weeds, I don't set foot in that thing again!...

Fine. Get it ready. Snowy and I are setting out again immediately!

Let's hope he doesn't run into any more trouble this time.

What shall I do? Tell him... or not?

I've made up my mind...

I... Captain... I've bad news for you.

Bad news for me?

No, bad news for you, very bad news... I'm afraid the UNICORN is not here... Look...

What's that gadget, eh?

Yes, it's a pendulum. I've taken up the study of divining, and I've arrived at the conclusion I just gave you...

All from that whatsit?

Yes, much further west ... You'll see. My pendulum will begin swinging from east to west... Look, it's started...

You see?... It's swinging westwards. The UNICORN will be found in that direction.

Look there, Captain! Smoke!

And look, there's the submarine surfacing!.. This time we've got it! ... He's found the wreck!

Have you found it?

Westwards... It's still westwards

Yes, I've found the UNICORN!... You can prepare the diving equipment!

You're sure you'll be all right? ...

Certain! I'll do everything exactly as you told me..

Good! Now, don't forget... If you want to come up, jerk the line twice... In an emergency, give a series of quick jerks.

Right!

Come on, pump hard!

We are!

?

Wooah! Wooah!

Wooah! Wooah!

That's it, he's touched bottom...

So this is the UNICORN!

Crumbs! What's happening? The air supply has stopped! ...

Thundering typhoons! What are you two doing there, instead of pumping?

Us? We're resting...it's tiring work, you know.

You infernal impersonations of Abominable Snowmen! Pump for your lives!...Faster!

Whew!...That's better! ...Now the air's coming again. That gave me quite a fright...

Excuse me, Captain, but I don't understand...Since the UNICORN is not here, why has Tintin gone down?

He's picking daisies down below!

?

Having a row? I don't see a boat?

Two jerks on the line! He wants to come up. I'm sure he must have found something!

Heave-ho!...Heave-ho!

Here he is

What has he got?

A gold cross, encrusted with precious stones!...and a cutlass!...I say, this cross is superb!

We've made a good start, eh?

Now why did he tell me that Tintin had gone for a row?

Yes, it's a good start. But this is nothing to what else we shall find. You'll see. I'm going down myself, this time.

By the way... er...any sign of sharks?

No, none at all.

Here's your helmet.

Good.

OW!... OOH! ... OW!

Whatever's the matter?

Blistering barnacles! My beard!

!

There, now your beard is inside.

Good. You can close my helmet now. Keep an eye on that pumping.

Aha! Now to find the treasure!...

A few minutes later...

A series of jerks!... The danger signal!...

Hurry! hurry! pull him up! ...Something frightful must have happened!

Let's hope that it's not a shark...

At last!

A bottle? What can that mean? ...

A bottle of rum, my friends! ... Jamaica rum, and it's more than two hundred and fifty years old! ... Just you taste it!

GLUG GLUG GLUG

GLUG GLUG GLUG

Mm!... It's wonderful!... It's absolutely w-w-wonderful! Y-y-you taste it!...Yes, yes, that's f-f-for you!.. I'm g-g-going st-st-st-straight back to g-get a-a-a-another f-for m-myself...

That beats everything! He's gone in without his helmet!

Billions of bilious blue blistering barnacles! Those two jelly-fishes forgot to pump again! ...

Sea-gherkins!... Freshwater swabs!.. Ectoplasms!... Bashi-bazouks!...

But...but it wasn't us, you ...

Silence! You were told to pump, then pump, by thunder!

It's no use drying yourself, Captain. You must empty your suit first... Take it off now.

Take it off?... Never!... Never!...

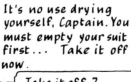

I'll rest a minute, and go down again ...

You see?... I told you so!... Your suit is full of water... We'll have to empty it.

There! Now you can go down again, if you still want to. But don't forget your helmet this time!

Off we go!... As for you, my hearties, just you keep on pumping until you're ordered to stop!... You understand?...

Yes, yes, we're pumping...

There he goes now...

The same evening...

A good day's work!... First that cross, and then ...more important, all this rum!... Fine stuff eh?

Yes, but I'd sooner have found the treasure.

Oh, we'll find that tomorrow, won't we Professor Calculus?...

Perhaps, but I'm inclined to think it is rum.

CHEEEP
CHEEEP CHEEEP

Ssh!

It sounds like a bird...

I'd say it was the squeak of a badly greased wheel...

CHEEEP

Let's see. I want to set my mind at rest.

There, Captain. It's the pump making that noise.

CHEEEP
CHEEEP

What d'you think you're doing at this hour?

You never ordered us to stop pumping, Captain. So here we are, pumping.

To be precise: we're pumping.

Off to bed, nitwits! You'll have plenty more pumping, believe me!

The next morning..

Something tells me Tintin is going to find the treasure this morning.

Another bottle of rum!... I'll leave it there for the Captain.

Hello, I wonder what we've got here?

A casket! Great snakes! Can it be Red Rackham's treasure?

I'll go straight up, and see what's inside this casket!

He's grabbed the casket!

Goodness, he's swallowed it! And he's coming back for me!

He's coming again. What can I do? If only I had a weapon.

Perhaps this bottle will help...

Quick, back against this old rib. Then he won't sever my air-pipe...

Good heavens, what a blow!

Thank goodness my suit isn't damaged.

?

My stars! He's drunk!

Now he's sleeping it off, I suppose. Here's my chance to try and recover the casket.

Two jerks on the line! He wants us to pull him up.

Heave-ho!... Heave-ho!... You wait! He'll be bringing us the treasure.

Thundering typhoons! Why does he have to struggle so?

?

Blistering barnacles, a shark! What a fellow; he's caught a shark!... But what does he want us to do with it?

The best thing is to ask him.

Of course!... Lower another line to him, and pull him up.

Now, up I go I wonder what the Captain will say!

Well, what's the meaning of this little joke?

Little joke?... Just cut open that shark, Captain, and you'll see.

In any case, I believe the fins are particularly tasty...

A few minutes later...

Captain!... Captain!... Look what we found in the shark's stomach!

A casket!... A casket!... Red Rackham's treasure!... Red Rackham's treasure!! ... Here it is at last!

Quick, into my cabin!

Hm!... Not so easy! It's all rusted up.

It's no good, you'll snap the blade. Better try this case opener.

Good idea. Hold it tight, you two.

Go on! Go on: don't worry, we're holding it...

CRACK

Got it!...

Billions of bilious blue blistering barnacles in a thundering typhoon!...It's not the treasure!

These are old documents, half eaten away by damp!

Documents? Fine! And what am I supposed to do with documents?

Come now, Captain, don't lose heart! ... We'll continue our search.

What's the use?

48

That's it!... I've got it!

These are old documents!... Definitely!... Old documents!

That chap will drive me crazy!

And you there? Thundering typhoons, what are you doing?

Me?... You can see – I'm helping my colleague to go down... Oh, don't worry. I've watched carefully how you do it...

What about the pump? The pump works by itself, I suppose?

I'll work the pump, nincompoop!... Then at least I'll know he's safe.

Thundering typhoons! What's that over there, on the deck?

The weighted boots!... He's forgotten the weighted boots!

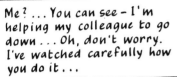

A fortnight later...

Here we are, pumping as usual...

As usual...

Blistering barnacles! You can stop pumping! Can't you see that Tintin's come up?

Well?

Nothing... Nothing at all! I've been carefully through all that's left of the poop...

It's just as I said: we aren't going to find it.

Come on, Captain, you ...

Tell me, what is that cross over there?

A cross? Where can you see a cross?

No, a cross... that cross over there on the is- land.

It certainly is a cross, isn't it? ...

I say, Captain, Professor Calculus is right! There is a cross, over on the tip of the island!

A cross?

You think so?

Thundering typhoons! It is indeed a cross!

Really? I'd have sworn it was a cross!

Hooray!... Hip-hip-hip-hooray!... I've got it!

?

Professor Calculus, Professor Calculus, you've saved us!

Let me waltz ♪♪ with you ♪♪, The whole ♪♪ night through ♪♪

Quickly, Captain!... Picks!... Shovels!... We're going back to the island.

Yes, Captain, the treasure lies there! You remember the words in Sir Francis Haddock's message: "then shines forth the Eagle's cross". There it is: the Eagle's cross!

Thundering typhoons! You're right!

Hooray! Thomson!... Thompson!... Fetch the picks and shovels! Hurry up!...Into the dinghy!

Well, Professor Calculus, we can never thank you enough!

It is rather rough..

No, I said it is thanks to you that we are going to find the treasure.

Oh... Well, I'm sure it's a cross!

Of course, of course it is a cross..

No?... D'you think so?

Baboon! Fresh-water swab!

Hello, my old friend!

Hooray! Here it is!

Gentlemen, this is it, the Eagle's cross!

Well, what did I tell you? Is it or is it not a cross?

Why, what's the meaning of all these notches?

A calendar! When your ancestor was marooned-like Robinson Crusoe, he counted the days until he was rescued. Look: there's a small notch for weekdays, and a large one for Sundays...

To work, to work! I'll give a bottle of rum to whoever finds the treasure!

Are you... er... looking for something?...

!

Blistering barnacles, put away your pendulum; come and give us a hand instead!

Towards the west; yes, it does...

What can they be searching for like that?

But... no, it's impossible!

What?... What is so impossible?

That the treasure can be here!

W.w-what?... Why?...

Just think... Supposing Sir Francis Haddock left the UNICORN, carrying the treasure; why would he have buried it here, at the foot of this cross?... What would you have done in his place? On the day you left this island you'd have taken the treasure with you, wouldn't you?

But then...

Then?... Probably the treasure is still out there, under the sea!... And we've followed a false trail!

All because of that creature Calculus, blis- tering barnacles!

Yes, it's all your fault, you certified ignoramus!

Yes; I'm tired of telling you: it's further westwards!

Westwards!... Westwards!... I'll give you westwards!

OH!

Now your infernal pendulum's gone west, you Olympic athlete, you!

Wooah! Wooah!

Take that!... And that!... Now it's buried, pestilential pendulum!

There!... And don't mention it again! Come on now, we're going back!

He's furious!

What a good little doggie you are!...

Down, Snowy!...No more games, now!

Is something bothering the Captain?...He seems to be rather worried!

Where have the Siamese twins got to?

Why, I thought they were behind us.

AHOY! THOMSON! THOMPSON!

No, no, please don't worry. The little dog brought it back for me.

Billions of blue blistering barnacles! This time I've had enough!

Captain! Captain!

Leave me alone! I've got to let fly at something!

Thousands of thundering typhoons! That's the lot, eh?

53

Now, Captain, you sit down while I go and have a look for those two...

All right.

I wonder where they've got to, the sillies!

Where has Tintin gone?

He's gone west!

I think I can hear them.

What on earth are you doing here?

Us?... We're filling in this hole... It's safer... People never look where they're going...

Next day...

Well, you've quite made up your mind to go on searching?

For a few more days, Captain. Look, today is the 9th. If we haven't found anything by the 15th, we'll give up the game and go home...

Just as you please...

You won't regret it. And it will give us a chance to try and raise some of the remains of the UNICORN... The figurehead, for instance.

Off we go! Pumping again!

Here's to the 15th when we'll be able to stop! I'm fed up with this business..

Come to think of it, I haven't seen Calculus today. Is he ill?

10
THURSDAY

11
FRIDAY

What's up with Calculus? He's not left his cabin for three days.

12
SATURDAY

13 SUNDAY

Still no luck, Captain...

14 MONDAY

15 TUESDAY

?

What... What's happening?... It looks as if...

Oh dear, I'm right! ...I must warn the Captain!

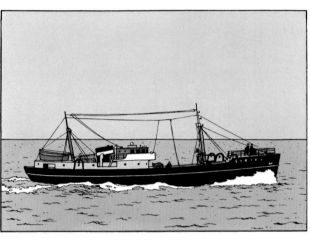

Come on, Captain, don't let this upset you. It's bad luck, I know, but you must make the best of it...

Captain!... Captain!... The ship is sailing!

Well, what would you like it to do? Dance a jig?

Ah, I see now. At last you have realised that the UNICORN is not where you were looking; you are steering westwards. I understand..

I've had enough! Come with me!

You see that, eh? I suppose it's the figure-head of the TITANIC!

My word, it's a unicorn! But what about my pendulum, which swung to the west?... How extraordinary...

16 WEDNESDAY **17** THURSDAY **18** FRIDAY **19** SATURDAY **20** SUNDAY **21** MONDAY **22** TUESDAY

RRRING
RRRING

JULY
23
WEDNESDAY

Hello. Yes... "Daily Reporter" ...Yes...What? The SIRIUS has docked?...Are you sure?... Good... Thanks!

Hello, is that you Rogers?...Go to the docks at once. The SIRIUS has just come in...I want a good story about her!

Well, Captain, I'll say goodbye to you now. I'll have my submarine collected tomorrow morning.

All right. Good.

Now, please let me thank you, Captain. You have been so very kind.

Oh, it was nothing.

Yes, yes, Captain. Thanks to you, I shall always have unforgettable memories of my stay on board...

So shall I!

THUD

Er... excuse me...I missed a step!

Allow me to introduce myself: Ken Rogers of the "Daily Reporter"

"Daily Reporter"? Wasn't yours the paper that gave the news of our departure?

It was!...And we would like to publish a sensational article about your trip. May I ask you a few questions?

Of course...

I'm rather busy myself. This is my secretary, Mr. Calculus; he will be happy to answer all your inquiries.

Delighted...

Now Mr. Calculus, about the treasure...

Oh yes.

I'm sure you have it there, in that suitcase...

Thank you, I'll carry it myself.

I can understand that!...Now tell me, what does the treasure consist of?

No?... Not really?...

No, I asked you what was in the treasure you found. Was it gold?... Pearls?... Diamonds?

Incredible! I don't believe a word of it!

56

Look, Mr. Calculus, I don't quite follow...

Of course! But let me give you a little advice: don't tell anyone!

And you may rely on me – I will keep this strictly between ourselves!

Well, Captain, our mission is completed. Because he knew we were aboard, Max Bird didn't dare interfere with your activities.

No doubt... You're going home now?

No, we're a bit tired... The journey, you know... and the pumping... We're going to spend a few days in the country with a farmer friend of ours.

Have a good holi---day!

Now for the simple, healthy tasks of the countryside! No more pumping!

To be precise: no more pumping!

... and when you've finished crushing the oats, you can have a turn at the chaff-cutter.

Some days later...

RRRRING

Good morning, Tintin.

Hello, Professor Calculus. What brings you here?

Very well, thank you. And you?... I've come to bring you the documents...

The documents?... What documents?...

No, the documents we found in the casket... Don't you remember?... I've tried to piece them together, sticking the fragments on sheets of paper. Some are illegible. Others, like that one, are comparatively easy to decipher.

I believe that one will interest the Captain particularly.

Great snakes! I think so too!

Come on! We must see the Captain!

Charles the Second, by ye Grace of God King of England, desiring to reward Our trusty and beloved Knight, Francis Haddock... Blistering barnacles!

The rest! Read the rest!

Thundering typhoons! Am I dreaming! It's Marlinspike Hall!... Marlinspike, my family estate! It's fantas-...-tic!

But you don't know the latest! Wait, you'll see...

Here... read this!

Well, what about that?

PROPER...

JAMES BIDDUP & CO.

For Sale by Auction

ON SATURDAY, 9TH AUGUST

MARLINSPIKE HALL

This magnificent, beautifully appointed, and historic residence ...tensive parkland and

What about it?... Well, Captain, it's quite simple. Your family estate is for sale?... You must buy it back!

Buy it back? With what?

That's true... We need some money.

Heigh-ho!... If only we'd found that wretched treasure, there'd be no question.

May I please have a look too?

Of course.

!

Captain, Marlinspike Hall is for sale!... Look! We must buy it back!

Oh, yes?

Buy it back?... That's easy, eh?... What about the money? I suppose you've got the money, eh?

Oh, yes, money!... That doesn't matter!..

That's all right! I have some money.

You? ... You've got money? ... That's nice for you! ... Personally, I haven't any!

Quite! The government have paid me a large sum for the patent on my submarine. Thanks to you I was able to try it out. Now it's my turn to help you ... Come along, we're going to buy your mans—ion.

HOUSE FOR SALE

This HOUSE is not FOR SALE

All's well that ends well! ... You haven't found the treasure, but you have got back your family estate.

It is magnificent!

Wait, you haven't seen anything yet.

This is the room where I telephoned you.

Splendid!

SSH!

No ... Nothing ... I thought I heard footsteps ...

Oh?

Well, it's a wonderful house! ... My ancestor had good taste, didn't he? ... Now what about those famous cellars you talked of? Where are they?

Come with me ... I'll take you there.

Look! Here we are!

Thundering typhoons!

What a lot of junk!... All this junk!

Oh yes, the Bird brothers used this as a storeroom.

Look, that's St. John the Evangelist. We must be in an old chapel...

What do you think of it?

Incre... dible!

Sh!... This time I'm sure I heard a noise...!

It's gone... The footsteps have stopped... It's queer. I wonder...

What?

Why, whatever's the matter? What is it?

Hooray!

The Eagle's cross!... "And then shines forth the Eagle's cross"! There it is... the Eagle's cross...

The Eagle's cross?... I can see a cross, but where is the Eagle?

There, in front of you!

Yes there, look!... St. John the Évangelist – who is always depicted with an eagle... And he's called the Eagle of Patmos – after the island where he wrote his Revelation... He's the Eagle!...

There's a globe!

And an eagle!... You're right! ...

There, just on the spot given in the old parchment, is the island we went to!... Great snakes! The island's moving!

?

!?

*!?

The treasure!... The treasure!!... Blistering treasures! It's Red Rackham's barnacles!

We've found it!... We've found it at last: Red Rackham's treasure!... Look! ... Look!

It's stupendous!... Stupendous!... So Sir Francis Haddock did take the treasure with him when he left the UNICORN... And to think we were looking for it half across the world, when all the time it was lying here, right under our very noses...

Thundering typhoons, look at this!... Diamonds!... Pearls!... Emeralds!... Rubies! ... Er... all sorts!... They're magnificent!

Sh!... Did you hear that?

Yes...

Listen... Footsteps! ... Someone's coming towards the cellars ...

Quick! Get hold of a weapon! We'll each hide behind a pillar...

Right! Come on!